The 13 Pet Geists

By Rose Anderson

Illustrations by
Jean-Baptiste Tournay

The 13 Pet Geists

Published by RoseKnows Inc.

P.O. Box 5448, McLean VA 22103-5448

ISBN 0-9755889-0-7 (trade)

0-9755889-1-5 (library)

Library of Congress Control Number: 2004094655

The 13 Pet Geists! Quirky, playful, lovable animal ghosts!

You're off to the Geist Reserve, the enchanted afterlife home for animals! Here, the 13 Pet Geists live, work and play together. They cook, sew, sing and build, just like you and me. But everyday is a crazy day with these high-spirited animal ghosts. Whether they're playing together or visiting the living animals they call the "Livies," wacky things can happen, and usually do. The 13 Pet Geists are so much fun they'll become your favorite pet ghosts!

The ghostly wild fun has just begun!

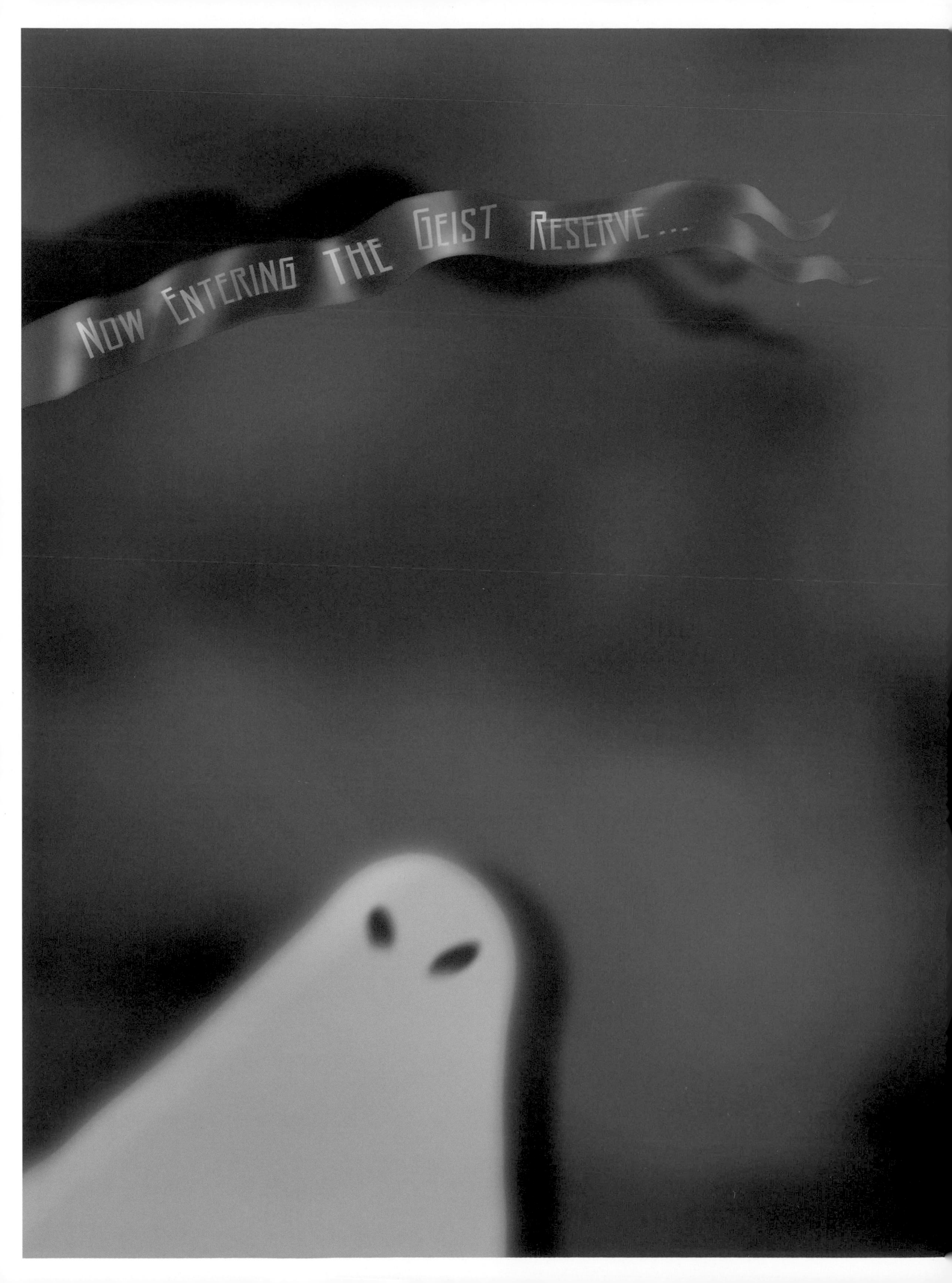
Now Entering the Geist Reserve...

Sami the Geist Crocodile

Who's got the most teeth? Are you wondering who?
Sami has three times as many as you.
He has ninety-nine teeth, the whitest you'll see.
That's three times your teeth, really three times plus three!

No one likes dentists, as everyone knows.
Being poked in the gums is not fun, I suppose.
But Sami the dentist is one of a kind,
And if you go see him, you might change your mind.

The Pet Geists love Sami the Geist crocodile.
They say they go see him to fix up their smile.
But they actually like to spend time in his chair!
I'm sure you'll agree that it's really quite rare.

Check-ups at Sami's are easy to take.
You'll be laughing so hard that your belly will ache!
He's quick with his jokes, the quickest they say,
Still quicker with tricks on his trickiest day.
And throughout your check-up, he makes it all fun.
Before you stop laughing, your teeth are all done!

He's got a big knob on the top of his snout,
And all sorts of strange funny sounds can come out.
Like wisses and hisses and bellows and grunts!
The wackiest sounds for his wackiest stunts!

"It's okay to play," our Sami would say,
"As long as you brush at least two times a day.
And remember to floss in between all your teeth.
A long skinny mouse tail works best underneath!"

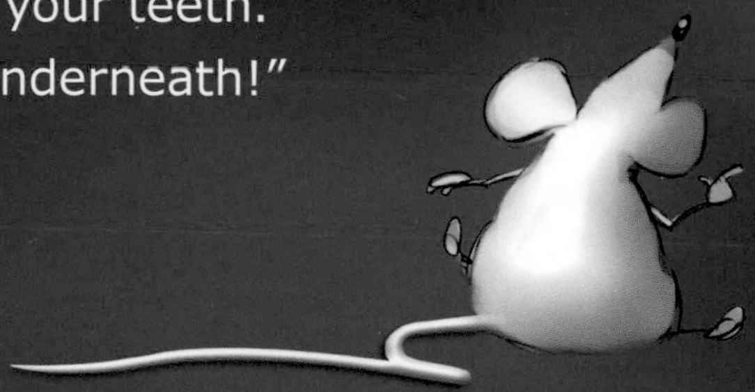

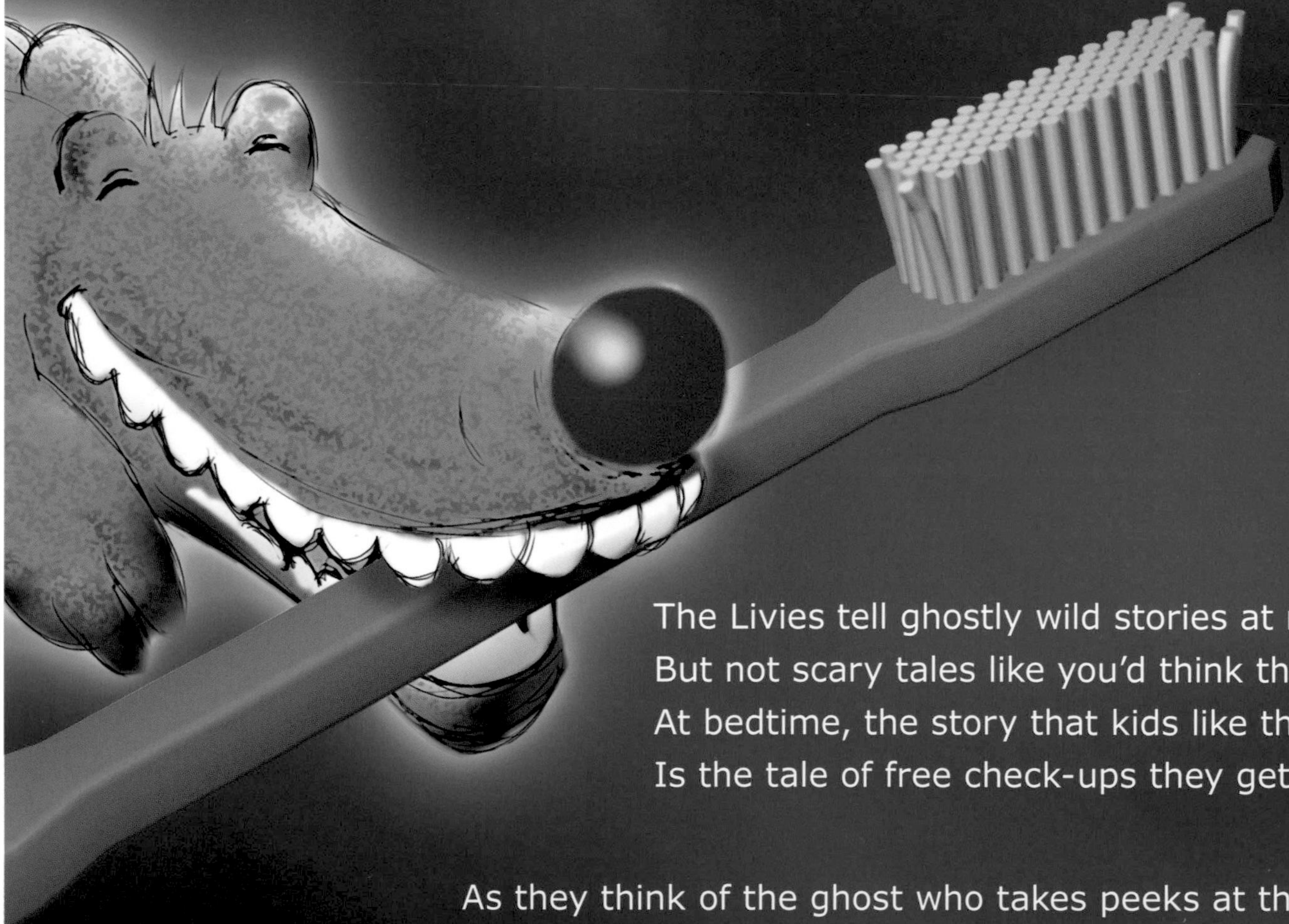

The Livies tell ghostly wild stories at night,
But not scary tales like you'd think that they might.
At bedtime, the story that kids like the most
Is the tale of free check-ups they get from a ghost!

As they think of the ghost who takes peeks at their teeth,
The kids pull up their blankets and giggle beneath.
"But who's this teeth peeker?" they ask with a smile.
Just ask any Pet Geist, they've known all the while,
It can only be Sami the Geist Crocodile!

Twiga the Geist Giraffe

TWIGA THE GEIST GIRAFFE

Any other Pet Geist looks just like a speck,
Looking down from atop our giraffe builder's neck.
Above the Reserve at twenty feet tall,
He's clearly the tallest Pet Geist of them all!

As a baby, he always was bumping his head.
"I'll build things much taller when I'm older," he said.
He dreamed of tall buildings that soared up so high.
Way over his head, they would reach for the sky!

You'll never see Twiga be lazy or shirk.
He likes being busy. That's his special quirk.
So Twiga's favorite time of the year
Is when all the mighty Geist rhinos appear.
Buildings get trampled. It's quite a stampede!
Then Twiga gets busy, rebuilding full speed!

While he works, Twiga sings, "If you put up a wall,
Make sure that your wall is the tallest of all!"
When Sami asks Twiga how tall his should be,
He replies with a smile, "Why, tall enough for me!"

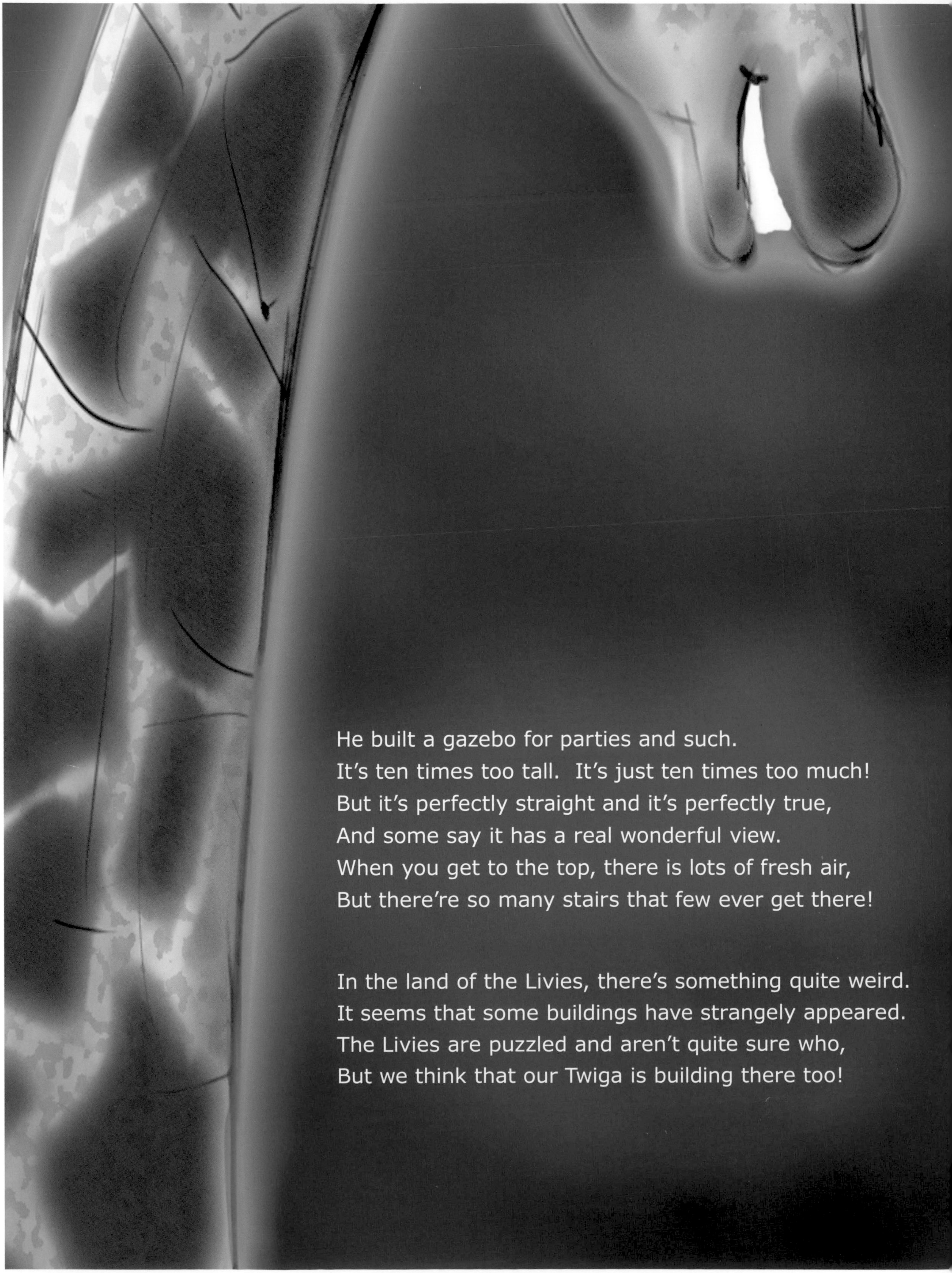

He built a gazebo for parties and such.
It's ten times too tall. It's just ten times too much!
But it's perfectly straight and it's perfectly true,
And some say it has a real wonderful view.
When you get to the top, there is lots of fresh air,
But there're so many stairs that few ever get there!

In the land of the Livies, there's something quite weird.
It seems that some buildings have strangely appeared.
The Livies are puzzled and aren't quite sure who,
But we think that our Twiga is building there too!

Mutu the Geist Chimp

MUTU

THE GEIST CHIMP

He chops with his hands and he stirs with his feet.
He whips up great food without skipping a beat.
This playful and cute acrobatic*al* imp
Is Mutu the chef, the award-winning chimp.

His all bugs and slugs buffet is the best!
They gave him two medals at the cooking contest.
The gold for his Fleas and Fruit Flies Flambé.
The bronze for his soft slimy Sea Slugs Soufflé.
Winning two medals was such a big thrill
That he cart-wheeled and tumbled and flipped down the hill!

Mutu as chef means great suppers at night,
And wonderful breakfasts and lunches cooked right.
Sometimes he spices the Livies' food too.
The Livies enjoy it, but they don't have a clue!

Our cook has some very big hungers to please,
But grocery shopping for him is a breeze.
He gathers his food while he swings in the trees,
Using the vines like a circus trapeze.
He says, "Cooking with two hands is really a blast!
Try adding your feet and it goes really fast!"

His kitchen is noisy, real noisy they say,
With crashes and bangs and loud "Hoo Hoos" all day.
And he calls all the Pet Geists for supper this way:
"WRAAA!" It's so loud they can hear miles away!

There's no other cook that has his kind of flair.
He waves and he twirls his long arms in the air.
"Voilà!" he exclaims. "My best dish I declare!
A masterpiece! No other dish can compare!
Tarantulas 'n Cheese with crumbled honeybees!"
It wows everyone and the Pet Geists say, "Mutu ... please,
Can we have extra bees on our 'Tulas 'n Cheese?"

Rumbo Jumbo
the Geist Elephant

RUMBO JUMBO
THE GEIST ELEPHANT

The Pet Geists gave Rumbo his "Jumbo" nick-name.
If you happen to see him, you'll do just the same.
Twenty-one lions can't equal his weight,
Nor two big full hippos right after they ate!

His trunk is real handy, incredibly strong.
His trunk is much longer than seven feet long.
It's springy and swingy with fingers that grip.
It's like a spare hand on his trunk at the tip!

His long twitchy tail flicks mosquitoes away,
And big pesky flies in the heat of the day.
His great big old ears are another neat tool.
They flap-flap all day so they help keep him cool.

Rumbo the Jumbo does moving and hauling.
He's the first one they call when a roof top is falling.
He'll pick up and move all your valuable stuff,
Or help out a friend when the going gets tough.

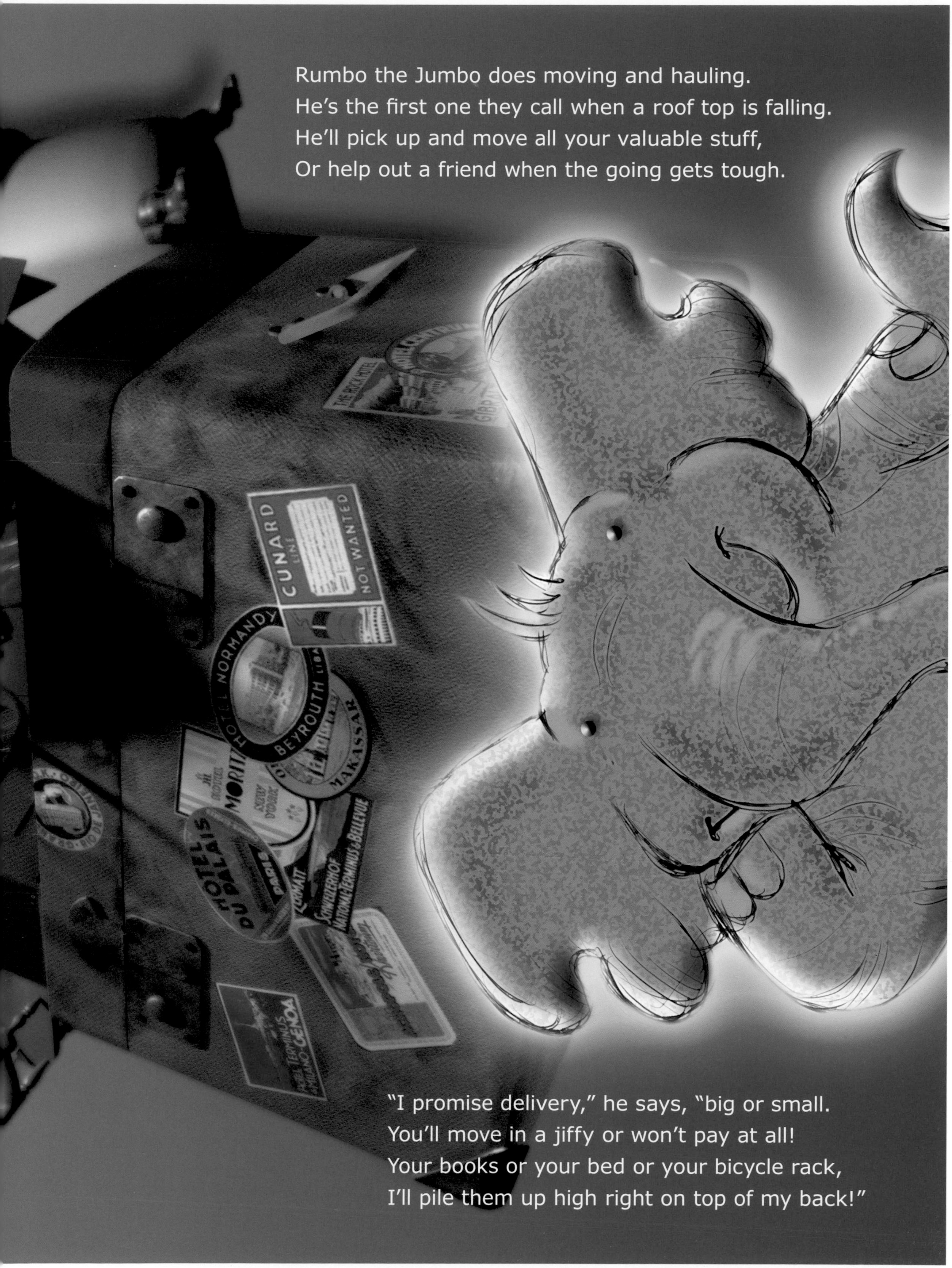

"I promise delivery," he says, "big or small.
You'll move in a jiffy or won't pay at all!
Your books or your bed or your bicycle rack,
I'll pile them up high right on top of my back!"

He moves for the Livies, like it or not.
Once, he moved all their stuff but where to, he forgot!
Where their piles of stuff went, the Livies can't guess,
But at least they got rid of their junky old mess!

Our Rumbo is huge, and boy can he eat!
Always filling his tummy with some kind of treat.
When he moves all your stuff, he won't ask you for money,
But he'll ask for your fruit, and for all of your honey!

The Pet Geists hide food and you may wonder why.
He once gobbled up the Reserve's fruit supply!
He kicked and he bumped and he knocked the tree trunks,
Then scooped up the fruit and the coconut chunks.
He blew great big gusts through his trunk way up high,
And knocked down papayas as easy as pie.
So now you all know that's the real reason why.
You'd hide your food too if that Rumbo walked by!

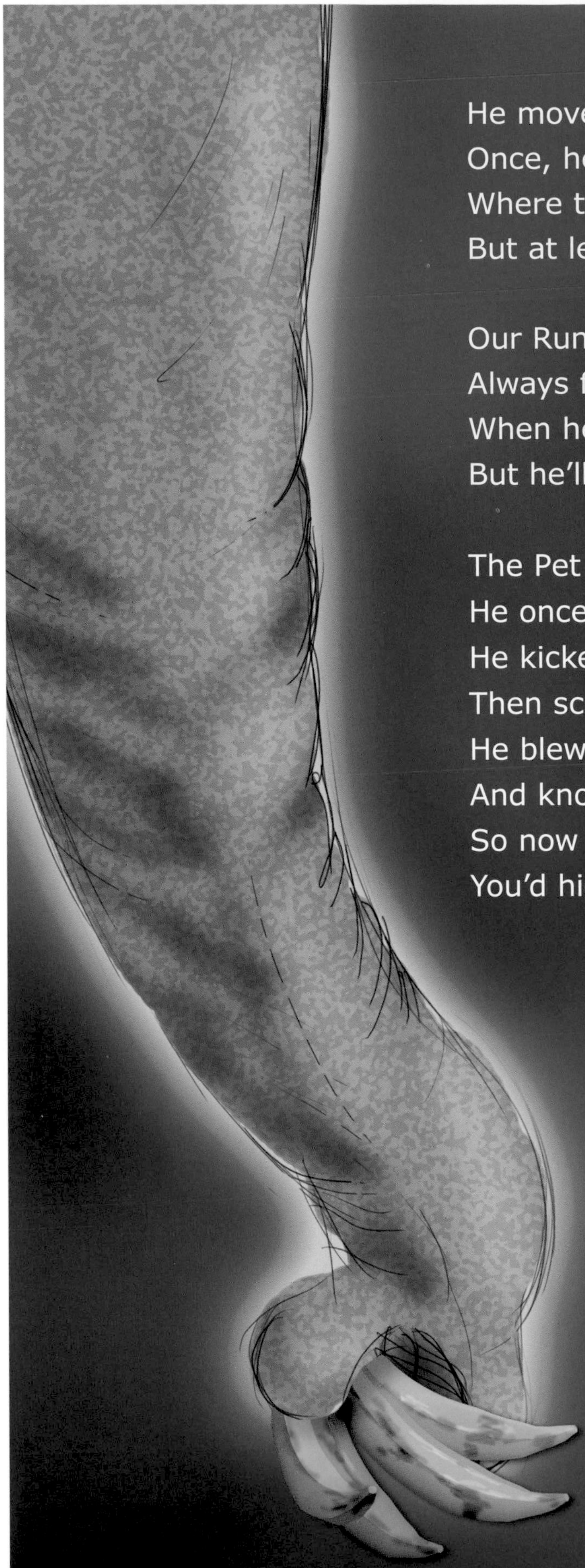

Kiboko the Geist Hippo

KIBOKO
THE GEIST HIPPO

The Reserve has a hippo that sings everyday,
But her shrieks and her screeches might scare you away!
Cups start to shatter and glasses will break.
The Pet Geists all scatter. Their ears start to ache!

But Kiboko the hippo is quite a sweet gal,
And when she's not singing, she's everyone's pal.
If someone is sad, she's the first with a hug.
She'll make you feel snug as a bug in a rug!

Set on short stumpy legs, her belly is wide,
So her little steps tilt her from side to side.
With small little ears, she can't hear all that well.
How bad is her singing? She can't really tell!

Her "La La La Las" begin early at dawn.
It wakes any Pet Geist with no earmuffs on.
To Kiboko, that's just warming up her great voice,
But the Pet Geists all wish they had some other choice!

Then she wallows in mud right on up to her chin
To give herself velvety soft silky skin.
"This mud bath," she says, "really helps keep me thin,
So I can look trim when my concerts begin."

At noon time she's never that far from a snooze.
She dreams of ovations and raving reviews.
This makes her wake up with a tune on her lips.
She stretches and yawns and then wiggles her hips.

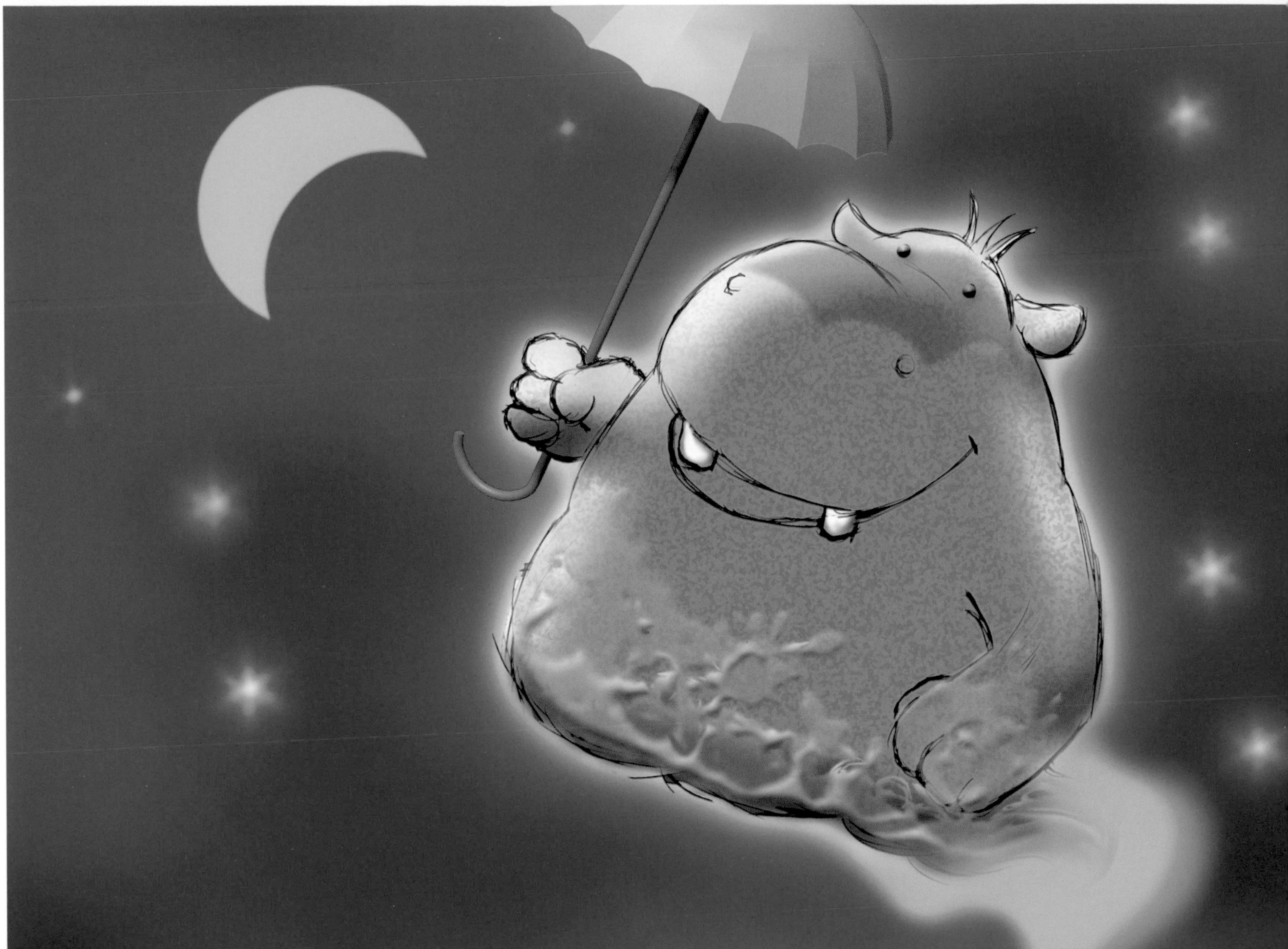

She longs to look up at her name in bright lights,
And give her friends magical musical nights.
"If I have an audience that's fit for a king,
Just think of the wonderful joy I can bring!"

She sings every night and still waits for the cheers
While the Pet Geists all run as they cover their ears.
Everyone loves her and they're her best friends,
As long as her dreadful and loud singing ends!

The Livies tell stories of ghosts wailing at night.
But the Pet Geists know better. They say, "It's alright,
Kiboko is loudest in the quiet moon light."

TUTTI THE GEIST TORTOISE

TUTTI THE GEIST TORTOISE

Tutti the tortoise tells fortune for all
With grasses and leaves and a big crystal ball.
This Geist fortune teller believes she can see
What you and your friends just might grow up to be ...
A pogo stick hopper or chopstick stick chopper,
A cheese pizza topper or popping corn popper!
It may sound all crazy. It may sound all nutty.
But some Pet Geists believe it, especially Tutti!

Tutti is old but her age doesn't show.
She's the first one who came to the Reserve long ago.
She's the world's biggest tortoise, at least that we know.
But at five hundred pounds, she's also quite slow.

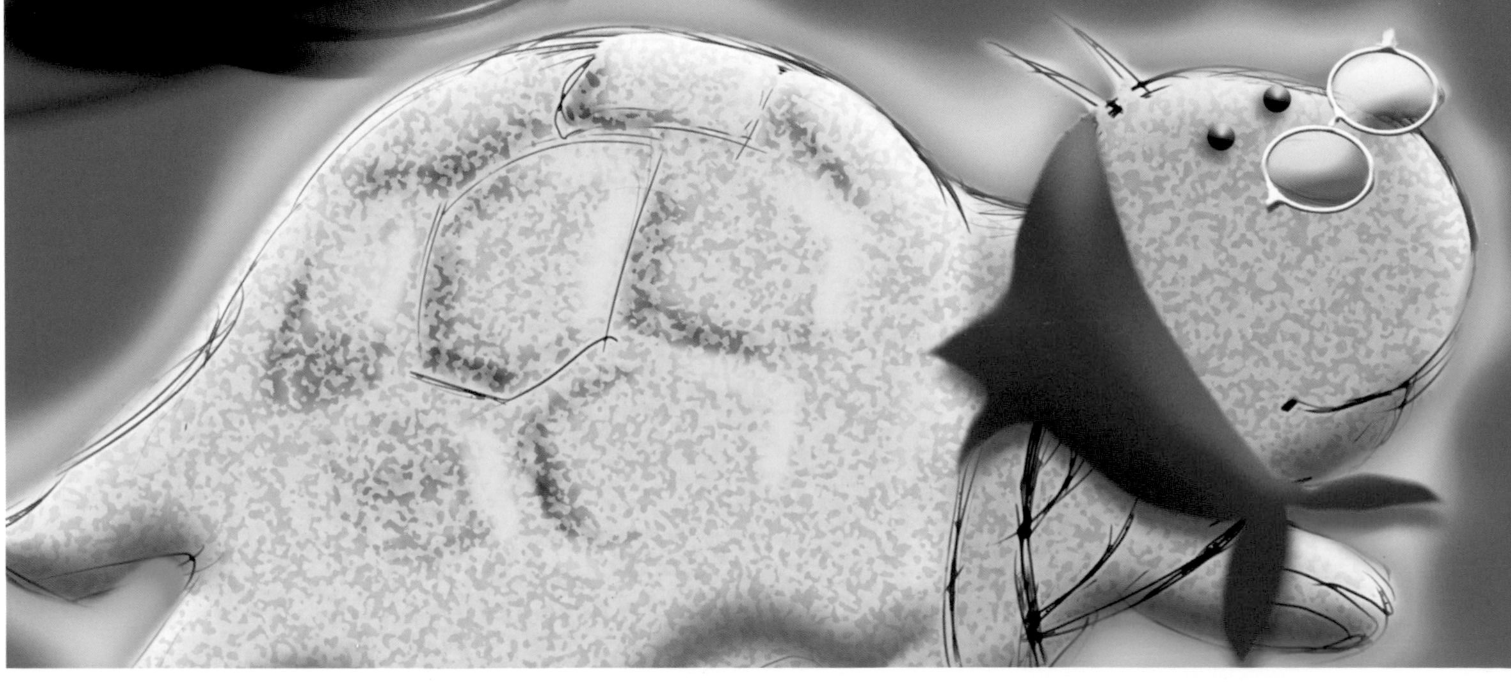

She gathers dead leaves and lots of dry grasses
To make psychic readings in small round eyeglasses.
She stands crystal balls on her nose really well,
And reads grasses and leaves in a coconut shell.

She claims she can see all the Pet Geists' lost past,
Or see how the lives of the Livies are cast.
But Tutti is neither correct nor that fast.
By the time that she tells you, your future has passed!

Once, she predicted a lingering drought,
But then the rains came and washed Twiga's homes out.
When she said her predictions will all become true,
They turned out to be wrong, except for a few.

"Her business is shaky," the Pet Geists will say.
Sometimes mad clients, they want her to pay!
So into her big yellow shell she will hide
By pulling her head, neck and legs back inside.

But though her predictions are often quite wrong,
No one stays mad at our Tutti for long.
'Cause Tutti is like the Reserve's old grandmother,
And the Pet Geists would not trade her for any other!

Paka the Geist Cat

PAKA
THE GEIST CAT

He swims and he fishes, so how about that?
He's Paka, the Reserve's own fisherman cat!

Paka learned that the water was not all that bad,
Baiting hooks all day long for his fisherman dad.
They caught every fish in the Sea of Japan!
That's when Paka's passion for fishing began.

As a little boy, Paka once broke his mom's rule.
He hid on a boat when he snuck out of school
To learn how to fish 'cause he loved it so much.
Then he found out he fished with a magical touch!

Most cats hate the water but not our Geist cat.
He knows that the water is where fish are at.
His two-layer fur keeps him from getting wet.
With a short and a long coat of hair, he's all set!

He has big dark round spots and his fur is light gray.
His camouflage makes sure he catches his prey.
You'll know it is Paka when you see him, they say.
Dark stripes on his forehead are dead giveaway.

Paka the cat is the strong silent type.
He likes being alone and you won't hear him gripe.
"Silence and patience catch fishes," he'll say.
"Don't talk, hawk or squawk 'cause it scares them away!"

He'll wait and he'll wait at the river bank's edge,
And dangle his paw from a flat rocky ledge.
Gently, he tap-taps the clear water top
To mimic a bug who just fell with a FLOP!
And when the big fishes come swimming nearby,
He lunges all claws as he grabs passersby.
No fish, big or small, has escaped Paka's snatch.
With claws and sharp teeth, Paka can't lose a catch!

He catches fish dinners for Pet Geists each day.
"We'll never go hungry with Paka," they say.
In fact, when the Livies feel hungry or blue,
Then one or two fish might appear for them too!
The Pet Geists all know who'd do something like that.
Can you guess who it is? Is it Paka the cat?

Bundi the Geist Owl

Bundi
The Geist Owl

When Bundi's inventions start up, you should run!
He builds them with everything under the sun.
With pulleys and levers and all sorts of springs,
Bundi the owl builds the wackiest things.
They're noisy, they clang and they bang with a clash.
They're flimsy, and often they fall with a crash!

So once in a while his contraptions go BOOM!
And scatter more messes all over his room.
If explosions don't knock him right out of his shoes,
Then Bundi would not get as much as a snooze.
'Cause Bundi works twenty-four hours a day,
If a knock on his head makes him nap, it's okay!

With loose and long feathers around his big head,
He's shaggy and looks like he's just out of bed.
His funny round face has these two big round eyes
Which always give Bundi this look of surprise.

But Bundi's keen ears pick up every small sound,
And his head can turn just about all the way 'round.
He's hard to sneak up on, but you would be too
If your head swivels 'round like an owl head can do.

He lives in his lab near a big shady tree
By the river, surrounded by junk and debris.
He works through the day and he works through the night.
His big round owl eyes let him work without light!

Well, Bundi is also a great handy-man.
If something needs fixing, our Bundi sure can.
If you bring him a broken up widget or two,
In no time, he'll get them all working like new.
But give him a chance and you bet that he'll add
More bells and more whistles than they ever had.
The crystal ball Tutti gave Bundi to glue
Came back with two wheels and was painted bright blue!
I'm sure you could say, "That's no reason to frown."
If your ball rolls away though, it will get you down!

But Bundi can't stop. He must fix what he finds.
The poor Livies think they have all lost their minds.
The Livies are baffled and can't quite explain,
But their things have been fixed, so they rarely complain.

Khai The Geist Lion

Ask Khai and he'll tell you he's not really vain.
He just happens to have both great beauty and brain.
That's Khai the Geist lion, the honorable mayor,
Who thinks he's the answer to any Geist's prayer.

You'll often find Khai by the shores of the brooks
Where the water shows clearly his dashing good looks.
"My whiskers," he tells, "are unequaled worldwide,
But my beautiful mane is my real joy and pride!"

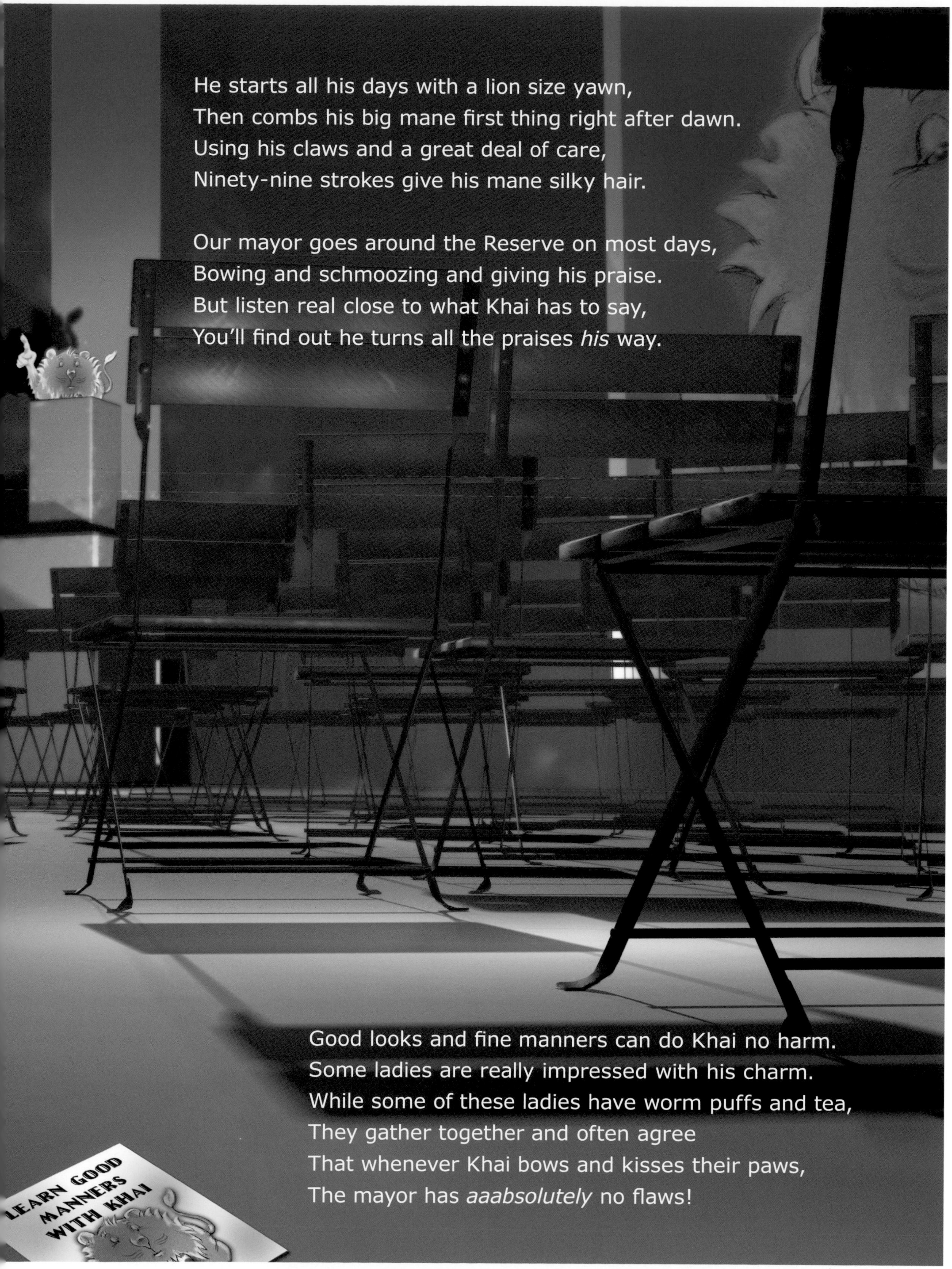

He starts all his days with a lion size yawn,
Then combs his big mane first thing right after dawn.
Using his claws and a great deal of care,
Ninety-nine strokes give his mane silky hair.

Our mayor goes around the Reserve on most days,
Bowing and schmoozing and giving his praise.
But listen real close to what Khai has to say,
You'll find out he turns all the praises *his* way.

Good looks and fine manners can do Khai no harm.
Some ladies are really impressed with his charm.
While some of these ladies have worm puffs and tea,
They gather together and often agree
That whenever Khai bows and kisses their paws,
The mayor has *aaabsolutely* no flaws!

LEARN GOOD MANNERS WITH KHAI

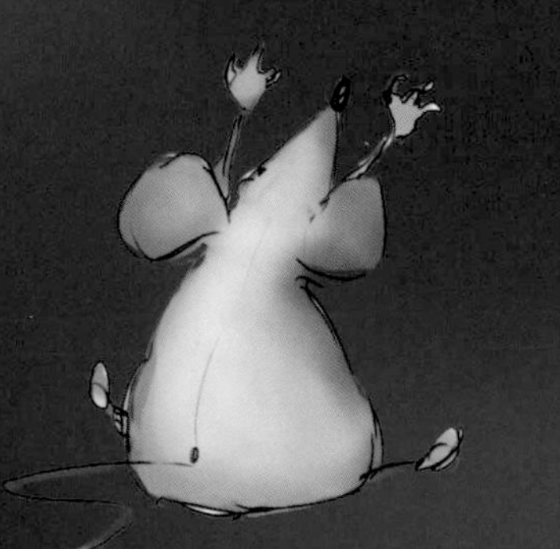

But some say our mayor is not all that hot.
Easily frightened more often than not.
He once gave a speech at a fancy affair.
A mouse that ran by scared him out of his chair!
Some ladies have said, "It's not true, it's a fable."
But it happened! He climbed right on top of the table!

But one thing for sure at which Khai is the best
Is giving his voters a well deserved rest.
'Cause whether he teaches or whether he preaches,
Our Khai likes to give really long-winded speeches.
The Geist parents won't ever miss them at night.
They speed up the snores so their babies sleep tight.
Can Khai bore the Livies to sleep quickly too?
The Pet Geists believe it. Now, how about you?

Punda Milia the Geist Zebra

Punda Milia

the Geist Zebra

Punda Milia the reporter is quick on her feet,
Covering news 'round the globe, or just down the street.
Give her a story, she'll never refuse.
Pet Geists or Livies, they're all in her news.

This reporter is nosey, and wow can she snoop!
She'll dig and she'll sniff till she gets a good scoop.
She'll snoop in your nest or your den or your coop.
She'll snoop in your broth or your stew or your soup!

e Reserve Tim

MYSTERIOUS DISAPPEARANCE OF ALL THE HONEY AT THE RESERVE

By Punda Milia - Staff Reporter

Is there a honey-thief among us? That's what the Geist Reserve residents want to know. "I was getting ready to make worm puffs when I realized all the honey pots were licked empty!" said Mutu the chimp, the famous chef. This reporter has learned that familiar large footprints were found at the scene. "It had to be someone with a huge appetite and big feet," said our mayor, Khai the lion. Expert trackers are following those footprints leading away from Mutu's kitchen. Anyone who can help solve the "Mystery of the Missing Honey" should contact this reporter at the Reserve Times.

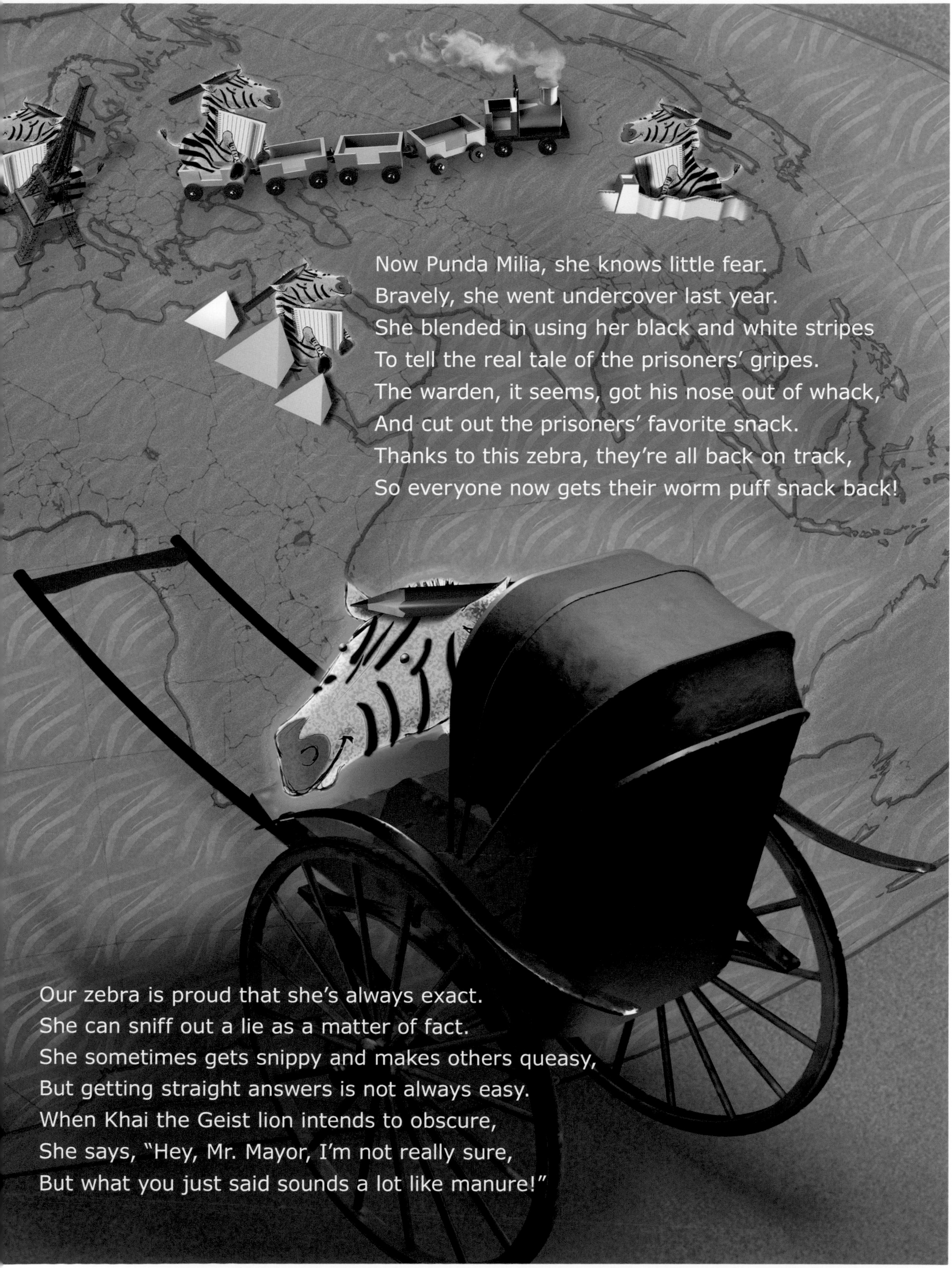

Now Punda Milia, she knows little fear.
Bravely, she went undercover last year.
She blended in using her black and white stripes
To tell the real tale of the prisoners' gripes.
The warden, it seems, got his nose out of whack,
And cut out the prisoners' favorite snack.
Thanks to this zebra, they're all back on track,
So everyone now gets their worm puff snack back!

Our zebra is proud that she's always exact.
She can sniff out a lie as a matter of fact.
She sometimes gets snippy and makes others queasy,
But getting straight answers is not always easy.
When Khai the Geist lion intends to obscure,
She says, "Hey, Mr. Mayor, I'm not really sure,
But what you just said sounds a lot like manure!"

Whether top story news, or the hot latest fad,
The Pet Geists all trust Punda's news, good or bad.
When Punda was named top reporter last year,
"Hip, hip, hooray!" the Geists let out a cheer.
"Thank you, oh thank you, that's so nice to hear!"
The overjoyed zebra cried out with a tear.
"My ears and my nose, I also must thank.
Without them, I would not be here to be frank.
I always can count on my zebra's good ear
That can perk up and turn, so I hear loud and clear.
And I always rely on my zebra's good nose
That can sniff out a rat just as well as a rose."

Popo the Geist Bat

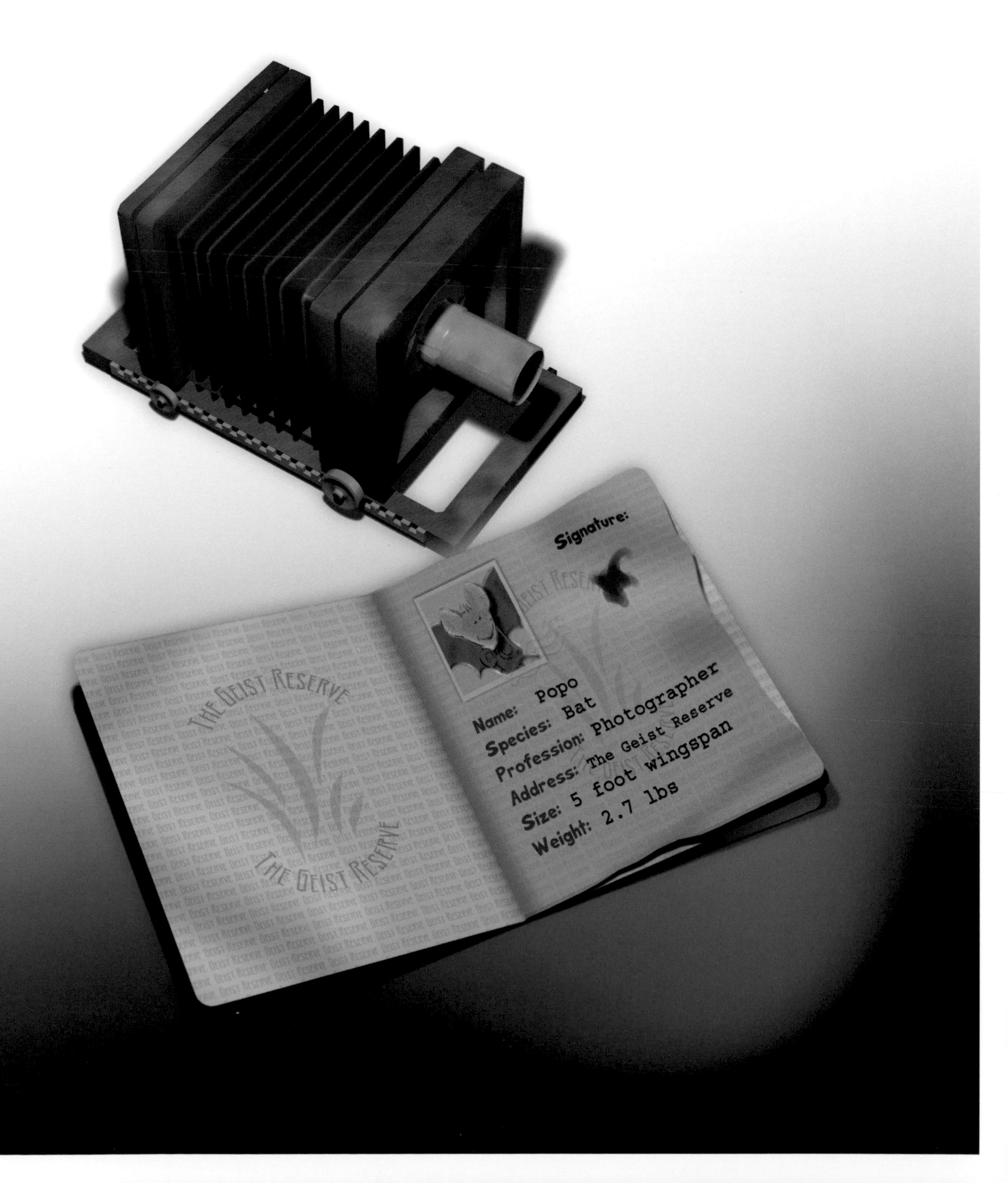

Popo the Geist Bat

Flap-ity-flap, Popo is flapping his wings.
Snap-ity-snap, he takes pictures of things.
He covers the Reserve from high above ground,
Snapping his pictures while flying around.

"I don't need fancy gizmos to focus," he said.
"My special bat sonar can focus instead!
To get a good shot, I just squeak out a squeak
That bounces right back to my ears so to speak."

His wings are like nothing that you've ever seen.
They're arms and long fingers with skin in between.
With wings like umbrellas, he swims through the air,
And steers with his tail while he flies here and there.

Fingers like Popo's would be pretty neat.
If yours were that long, they'd go down to your feet.
With a thumb and four fingers just like you and me,
He can hold onto things while he hangs from a tree.

Photographer Popo was just a small boy
When he found out a camera was his favorite toy.
It began when his mom on one bright sunny day
Said, "Here's your first camera, go outside and play!"

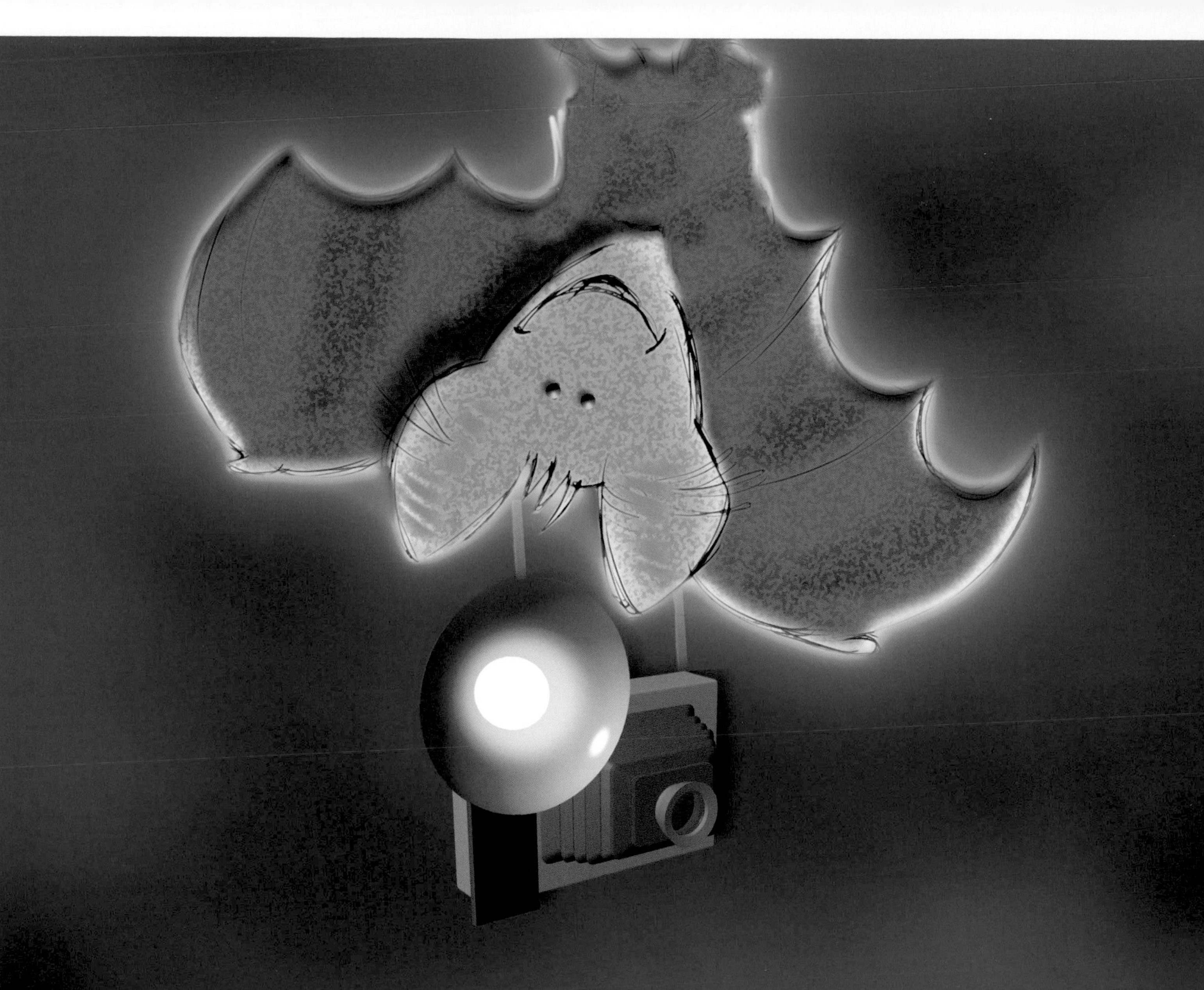

His family then moved to a big hollow tree
By a cave that's so dark inside no one can see.
He made it his darkroom. As soon as he did,
He was hooked! He was thrilled! He was one happy kid!

He began snapping pictures wherever he went
Of Pet Geists and Livies at every event.
Since photos like Popo's had never been tried,
In no time his pictures were published worldwide!

Khai says, "His shots are the best! His models are too.
My portrait is seen from Japan to Peru
On the front of a famous wildlife magazine.
I admit it's the best cover I've ever seen!"

Kipé the Geist Butterfly

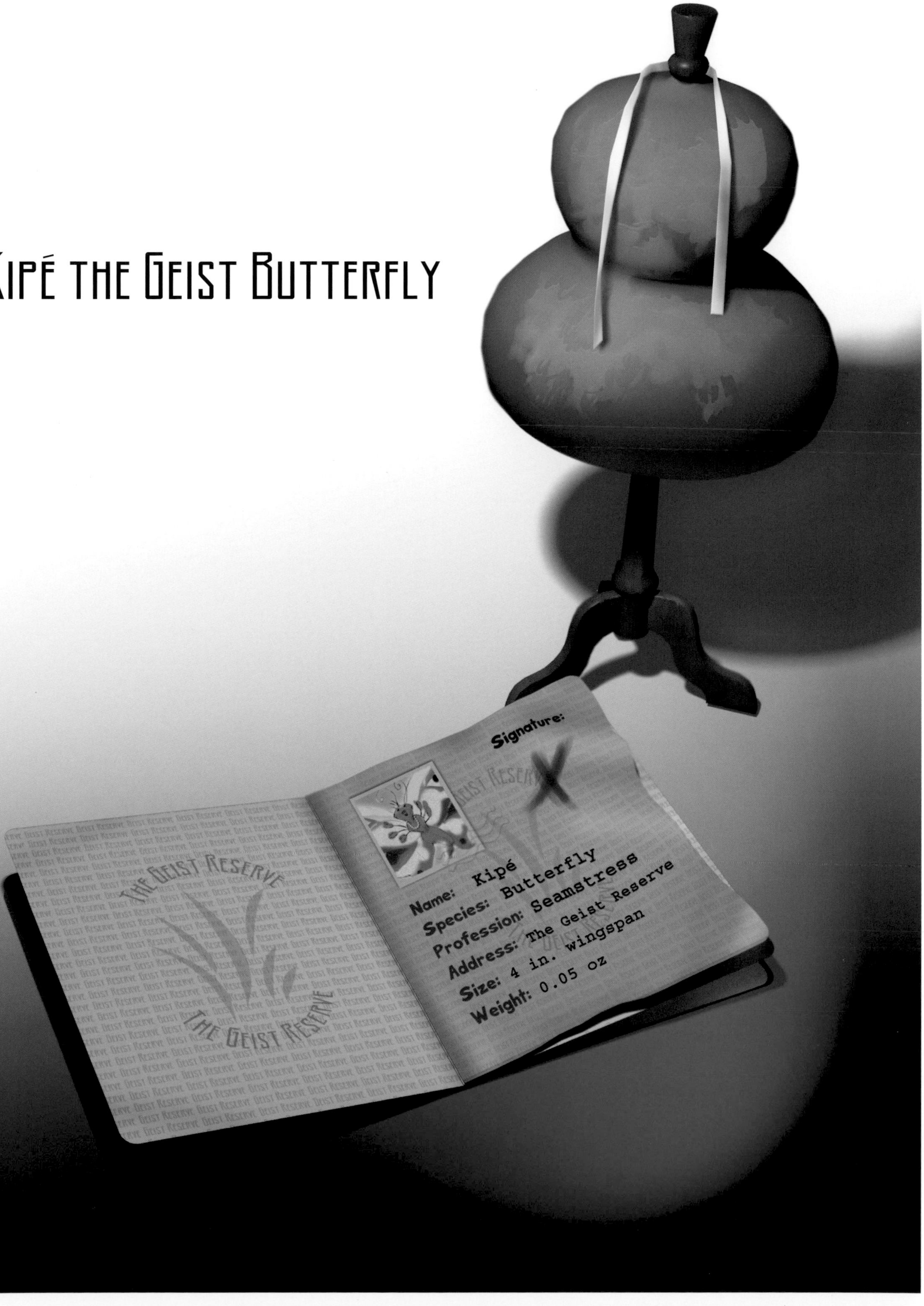

Signature:

Name: Kipé
Species: Butterfly
Profession: Seamstress
Address: The Geist Reserve
Size: 4 in. wingspan
Weight: 0.05 oz

The Geist Reserve

Kipé
The Geist Butterfly

To make sure your skirt is the cutest in town,
Or make sure your trousers won't ever fall down,
Call Kipé the seamstress, the Geist fashion queen,
And the prettiest butterfly you've ever seen.

The beautiful scales of her wings reflect light,
So her wings can change colors while she is in flight!
The Pet Geists all say, "She's so slim and so slight,
Only Kipé can make all these colors look right!"

Kipé the seamstress can sew with six feet,
Keeping her stitching real tidy and neat.
Top hats and gowns, she sews all sorts of things,
Guiding her needle by flapping her wings.

In one little second, her wings make twelve flaps.
Zip-ity-zip, a new dress out of scraps!
She'll stitch up a tux whenever Khai beckons.
Zip-ity-zip, in just sixty-six seconds!

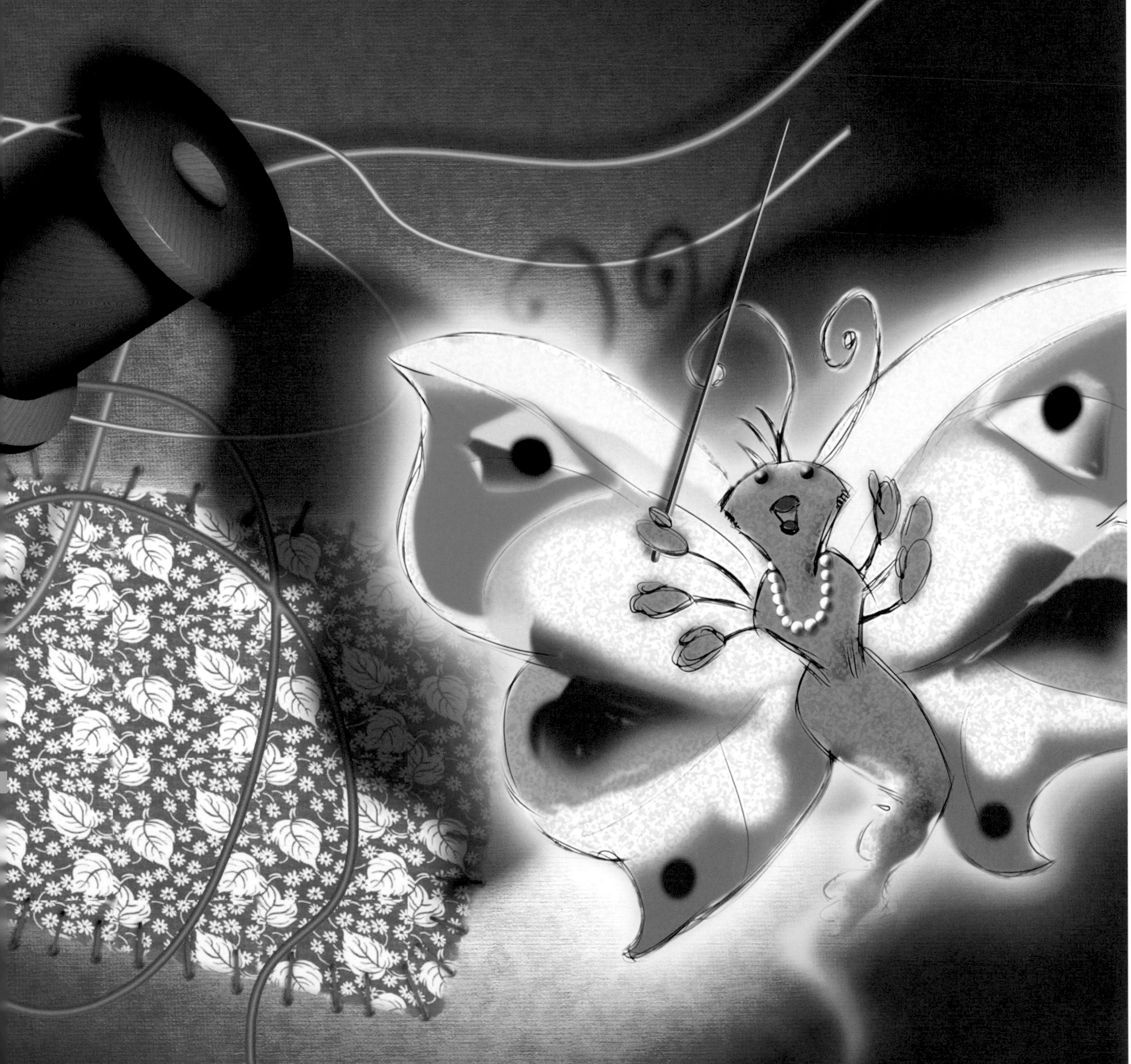

The Pet Geists won't make any bold fashion moves
Unless of course Kipé the expert approves.
Once Kipé said, "Pink is *sooo* out of style!"
Then Khai put away his pink tie for awhile.

The term "social butterfly" comes from Kipé.
She flits from one Geist to the next everyday.
They won't get a word in because she's so chatty.
She even drives Popo the Pet Geist bat batty!
She'll talk to the Livies who can't hear a word.
She just likes to talk and won't care if she's heard!

Kipé's big show is a yearly event.
It's a party. It's packed. It's inside a big tent.
But Kipé's last show is still talk of the town,
The kind of event she will never live down.
That's when Kiboko and Mutu both modeled.
Kiboko's first steps cracked the stage as she waddled.
Then Mutu decided he might as well swing.
Kiboko couldn't help it. She started to sing!
And yes, my dear friends, they collapsed the whole thing!

Nungu the Geist Porcupine

NUNGU THE GEIST PORCUPINE

"An earthworm a day keeps the doctor away,
But watch for his quills if you see him," they say.
The doctor is Nungu the Geist porcupine
Who never seems happy and just likes to whine.

Our porcupine nags about any old thing.
It's too hot in the summer, too cool in the spring.
Mutu's cuisine is not fancy. It's yucky!
The Livies are smelly. They're always so mucky!
Kiboko is noisy. She can't sing at all!
And Twiga's tall buildings are ten times too tall!
Paka likes fishes but who would want any?
And one Rumbo Jumbo is just one too many!
Kipé's new fashions are nothing but rags!
Nungu is cranky. He nags and he nags!

You want to know why Nungu seems like a grouch?
He can't scratch his back without yelling out "Ouch!"
He's covered with quills from his head to his toes.
He's covered with thirty-one thousand of those!

His needle-like quills, they lay flat on his back,
But they quickly stand up if you call him a quack!
Nungu's bad moods mean you'd better watch out,
'Cause porcupine quills can get stuck in your snout!

But who cares if the doctor is grumpy and prickly
When his wonderful cures work their magic so quickly.
He has potions and lotions for all of your ills,
Like fever and sniffles or colds, aches and chills.
He makes them with herbs and some strange little plants,
Adding black crawly critters like spiders and ants.
Even crickets or beetles and lizards go in.
Then he mixes them up in a bowl made of tin.

If Twiga the builder has twisted his neck
From building a house or a ten-story deck,
He makes him a lotion of ground-up fresh roots
With slug slime and grub grime and bright yellow fruits.
If Rumbo is sick with a big tummy ache
From eating too much of a ten-layer cake,
He makes him a potion of slimy fish guts
With pig tails and sea snails and fresh crunchy nuts.

At the Pet Geist Reserve, no one stays sick for long,
'Cause Nungu keeps everyone healthy and strong!